I0743080

S
F
BOOKS

SPARK & FIZZ BOOKS PRESENTS

PLANET SCUMM

AUTUMN 2018 "HUMAN RESOURCES" ISSUE NO. 5

AN ORGANIC TABLE OF CONTENTS

Planet Scumm is a triannual short fiction anthology. Visit **planetscumm.space** for submissions.

Portland | Boston | New York

Second Printing, 2019 ISBN: 978-1-970154-04-7

BIRDWAINER CORD

MISSION: SCUMM

We came to you because we heard you were the best. We came to you because you have a reputation for capturing targets alive. Most importantly--we came to you because we heard you have absolutely no sense of humor whatsoever. Did we come to the right bounty hunter?

Well?

I'll take that as a "yes." This data-cube thingy has the information on your quarry. It--no, no you have to stroke the purple crystal. Gentle, like a cat. A cat. Small furry friendly animal? Do y'all not have cats up here?

Sorry, we're still adjusting to the whole "galactic stage" thing. We're from Earth. What's left of it.

A *radio host*? Are these Earthers serious? Yeah, that's what I said Z3B. Easy money. Those weird little Earth rats better smarten up if they're going to make it without a homeworld.

Alright, better pull up the wire, see if this Scummy character's kicked up a trail somewhere.

Hmm, looks like Jackson Lewis Monk's sighted some old automated apartment units waking up on the far side of this galaxy. Could be our slimeball is looking to squat there and lay low. Psych profile says the guy isn't that fond of robot companions, though--not "squishy" enough. Better load "The Tower" into the case file anyway, Z3B. Just in case.

Now look at this. What would an intergalactic war criminal and inveterate party rocker like Scummy want with a bunch of office drones? John Rodzvilla's "Quarterly Report on Trans-Dimensional Holdings" claims some Earther-like folks the next system over have been experiencing bizarre cosmic-level phenomena. Worse, they're using their newfound powers for *capitalism.*

Hey, check this out—*another* Earther story making the rounds. Damn if they're not all over the place! This has to be our goo-man's doing. Richard Wren's got a first-hand account from a whole Earther planet where machines do everything, and the people can barely think for themselves. Now, don't look at me like that, Z3B. You're one of the good ones. I mean, you're *not,* you're a hardened killbot, but that's why we hang around.

More humans! And so far away from their former home... Just what did you do, Scummy? This transmission from Paul Spears looks like genuine history from just under a hundred years ago—at first glance. But even I know Earthers never developed the technology OR the interpersonal communication skills necessary to bottle concentrated emotional residue. Get "Ain't We Got Fun" loaded up too, Z3B, then punch it to our first lead.

Heh. Looks like this Scummy contract isn't a normal duty after all. Maker knows I haven't had a normal duty in ages. Don't tell anybody, but even after all these years I still like 'em hard and slow.

What's that Z3B? No, no, "duty." With a "U."

* Header Illustration by Natalie Pauline

PLANET SCUMM #5

HUMAN RESOURCES

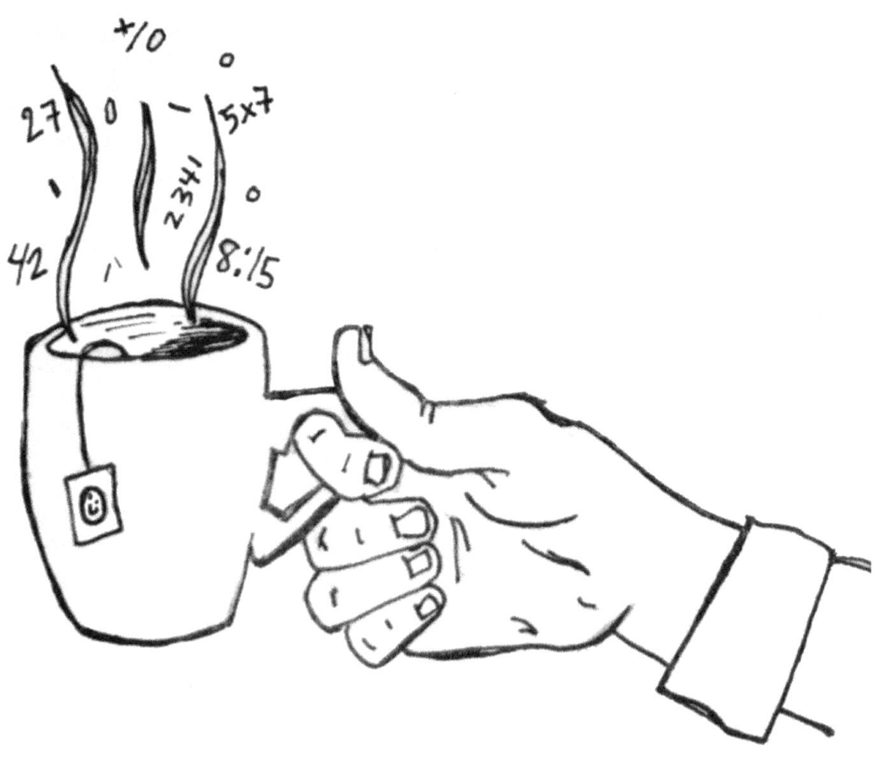

Spark & Fizz Books 2019
Portland | Boston | New York

AUTHORS

JACKSON LEWIS MONK doesn't exist. This is his first publication. You can follow his future work on Twitter: @jacklewismonk.

JOHN RODZVILLA teaches in the Publishing and Writing programs at Emerson College in Boston. His work has appeared in various publications including McSweeney's Internet Tendency, gorse, and The Literary Hatchet.

RICHARD WREN has been writing science fiction for the the last thirty years, on and off. He has worked as a science teacher and environmentalist for most of that time, both in schools and running an educational field centre and nature reserve. His stories have been published in Perihelion magazine, Nebula Rift and soon to be in Neo-opsis. Richard lives in the English countryside as close to the middle of nowhere as possible with his wife, daughter and menagerie of animals.

PAUL C.K. SPEARS is a novelist living in Boston. He enjoys video games, Pablo Neruda, and pondering whether fiction will keep us warm during the coming apocalypse. His first novel, Spirits of the Charles, is now available on Amazon Kindle and is coming out soon in paperback format. He has been published in Weirdbook Annual and Enter the Rebirth Anthology, among others. You can find him venting random strings of words on Twitter as @bostonspacejockey, or at Paul C.K. Spears on Wattpad, where his suspense fiction series, Mycenea, is barreling towards its surreal conclusion.

JACKSON LEWIS MONK

THE TOWER

The Tower would be an unimaginable sight to behold, if it weren't for the fact that no one has ever seen it.

It stands higher than any building has ever stood on this planet, piercing through the mesosphere. The red sun that hangs overhead casts a leviathan shadow on the sand beneath. The Tower, if any were there to gaze upon it, would seem to contain nearly every design and pattern that ever could be. The first hundred floors are all a bright, windowless steel design. Further up there are floors which jut out in all directions, floors covered in orange and paisley and wood pattern, that slant and slope, convex and concave. Floors which would bend the mind to even consider.

The Tower was intended to be a space-age domicile for the inhabitants of the former country it now stands in. Before anyone could enter it, life was struck from the face of the planet.

That is not to say that nothing inhabits the Tower. On the first floor the Greeter stirs from its chair, restless. It is a miracle of human labor, 200,000 years old and still it appears brand new. It closely resembles Man, with long metal legs, two shining arms, and a conical steel head which comes to a cruel point. Where its mouth would be--a speaker. It possesses one large red eye, which can scan, interpret, and store information. If a particularly poetic human were around, they might point out the symbolic link between the Greeter's eye, and the life-ending sun hanging in the sky. But no such human is there.

The Greeter walks briskly and pleasantly, in an organic, sauntering manner. Its feet click against the tiled floor one after the other, the sound of scraping treads ringing down the empty staircase at the end of its office.

The Greeter almost always stays on the first floor, in its Welcoming Office. Its purpose is to greet any visitors who come to its door, and to assign them a room. This has never happened. This weighs heavy on the Greeter's mind.

The Welcoming Office contains a small desk with a computer, several chairs, and a snack machine. The machine still contains a full array of snacks, kept at a perfect 50 degrees. The Greeter's most prized possessions are the several massive bookcases which line the walls of the office, containing classic literature on holographic print, as well as several classic movies. In the 200,000 years since its creation, the Greeter has read each and every one of these books and watched each movie time and again. The Greeter read and watched to prepare for its eventual guests.

The Greeter imagined it would go like this:

MAN

Hello fellow person, I would like a room to protect me from the harsh conditions outside.

THE GREETER

I can help you with that immediately! I must point out I am not a person, but am rather a sophisticated learning machine, here to assist you with all of your needs.

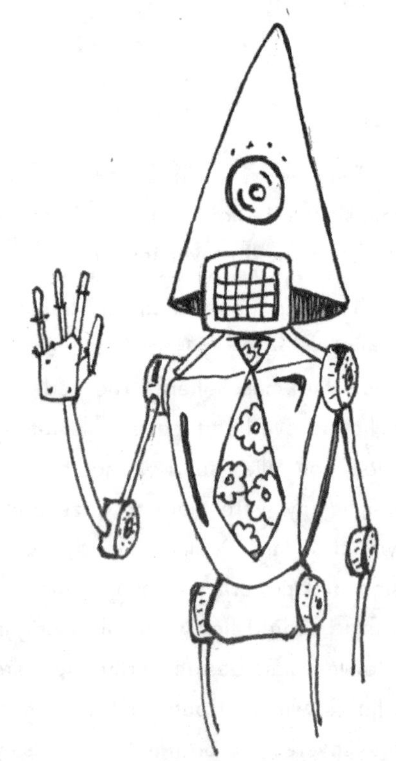

MAN

Oh my goodness! I apologize, you just seem so humanoid, with your two arms and two legs, and your friendly, calming voice!

THE GREETER

Thank you. While you wait for the Guide, would you like to discuss the work of Ambrose Bierce? Or maybe you and I could speculate together the contents of the suitcase at the end of *Pulp Fiction*?

THE MAN

That would be delightful. Might I add that you are performing your purpose superbly?

THE GREETER

Thank you. You too!

However, the Greeter is not imagining one of these conversations at the moment. Instead, the Greeter finds itself burdened with a terrible idea. Terrible ideas were surprisingly few and far between in the Tower, likely because only six conscious beings inhabit it.

Indeed, terrible ideas have been at an all-time low since the death of humanity.

The Greeter had been reading one of its favorites, *Nausea* by Jean-Paul Sartre. The novel closely follows, in journal form, the day-to-day of an author of history books, as he slowly descends into madness at the increasing futility of existence, and how sickening it is to be alive.

The Greeter, having no access to summaries, reviews, or discussions on the work it consumed, had previously understood this to be a comedy. "Look how Man," it thought, "In its infinite wisdom, supposed what it might be like to be me before I ever existed. Purposeless, without any pressing needs, having no effect on the world around me. How funny that this could be. Truly this displays how far-thinking Man is."

Today, however, that is not how the Greeter feels.

The Greeter, having no-one to express this terrible idea to, does the only thing it can do. It presses the bright, turquoise button marked "REPAIRS NEEDED." After a short eight months, the Mechanic appears.

The Mechanic is a multi-limbed wonder, an imposing dynamo of construction and repair. Its long, cylindrical body has fourteen jointed limbs, each displaying a variety of stupendous gizmos for the repair of its fellow automatons. It is made of a glamorous and durable blue alloy, a triumph of science and alchemy only just discovered before Man's demise. On top of its head, a dome sits with a flashing green light.

The Mechanic is simultaneously the most and least intelligent of the beings within the Tower. On one hand, it is so intimately familiar with the electric physiology of its compatriots that it could keep them all running indefinitely until the sun consumed the planet. On the other hand, that was just about all it could do.

"Erm, yes. Hello." The Greeter attempts to sound friendly, which should be simple. 'Sounding friendly', after all, was the Greeter's Man-given purpose.

"What seems to be the problem?" the Mechanic says in a grainy, pre-recorded voice--the extent of its communicative abilities.

"Yes, I... well I would like to call a meeting" the Greeter says.

"I'm sorry, I didn't catch that!" the Mechanic emits.

"A meeting! M-E-E-T-I-N-G." the Greeter spells, motioning its hands as though to push the words into the thick casing of the Mechanic's processor.

"I'm sorry, I didn't catch that!" The Mechanic repeats.

"Well then, the hard way I suppose" the Greeter says to itself. It opens a manual it had only just discovered last decamillenium in its desk.

"Ahem... Override Code 8417782AC dash ninety-three!" the Greeter pronounces in the hermetic manner of Merlin casting a great and terrible spell, its voice rising in occult excitement.

The light atop the Mechanic begins to flash red.

The Greeter orients itself in front of the communications system. It traces the button labeled "ALL CALL," a pseudo-organic excitement rising inside.

"This is..." the Greeter struggles for a moment, unsure what to call itself. "Me," it settles on.

"There is a problem with the Mechanic on Floor One, and I require all employees come down to the floor at once to discuss what is to be done. This is a Code 76139 dash Beta."

The Greeter waits. In a single decade, the other automatons are gathered alongside it.

Filling the perpetually empty space of the Welcoming Office stands The Guide, The Chef, The Maid, and The Architect. They are all upset, this minor inconvenience profoundly derailing the aimless work they busy themselves with.

The Architect, most powerful and important of the automatons, is the first to speak. It is little more than a walking computer, or rather a rolling computer. It is a foot high, six wheels underneath a ruby red cube with a small speaker on top. However, the Architect is connected digitally to the very foundation and structure of the Tower, able to build rooms and items at will, generated by the Tower itself. The Tower possessed some materialization capacity, which the automatons think they understand. None truly do.

The automatons had one previous meeting, 199,000 years prior, to discuss the problem of Man's apparent absence. The Architect had been the one to call it, and had spoken first there as well.

"Man has not yet come to the Tower, despite the grand opening being 525,607,800 minutes ago." The Architect said, in a tinny voice.

The other automatons had murmured in confusion.

"I have determined this to be a simple problem of imperfection. This Tower simply does not yet contain the necessary structures to provide for Man's wants and needs. I propose that we continue to perform and improve our functions indefinitely. I shall continue to add new floors, floors which might attract Man to this Tower. You shall all join in this joyous labor, and we will prepare a Tower so grand Man can not help but come to us." The Architect waited a moment, letting tension build in the room. 6 months later, once tension was sufficiently high, it punctuated this short speech with a slogan, one which would resound in the cybernetic minds of the residents of the Tower for millenia to come. "We can build this Tower into paradise."

An ecstatic cheer, vibrant and humming, had gone up.

That cheer is absent as the Architect speaks its first words since that day.

"Why have you called us here? How was the Mechanic broken? This should not be possible."

"Ah, yes, well," the Greeter paused. "I broke it. On purpose. I apologize, I needed to bring you here on false pretenses to be assured of your speedy arrival," the Greeter bashfully admits.

A murmur of disapproval rises from the other automatons, growing into a displeased choir of harrumphs and tuts.

"Why would you do such a thing? Have you malfunctioned?" The Maid inquires in its calm, quiet voice.

The Maid, being the automaton that most closely resembles Man, is somewhat shocking to look at. Man, when designing this Tower, had decided to make the Maid look entirely human, and so it possesses a skin-like polymer over its body, resembling an attractive woman. It wears a cliché maid outfit, which to the other automatons seems like an official uniform. This covering of polymer flesh and resplendent cloth grants the Maid a certain air of nobility, which frightens and enthralls the other automatons.

"No! No. At least I do not believe so. I merely have been thinking, and wanted to share my thoughts with you, my fellow...my fellows," the Greeter stammers out in reply.

This takes a moment to sink in, and some days later, the Guide speaks.

The Guide is a floating spectre, a cloud of information and noise projected by the Tower. It flickers near the ceiling of the Welcoming Room, peering down on its compatriots. The most ethereal of the automatons, it seems to the others as though the Guide is the voice of the Tower itself.

"What in all of this Tower are you talking about, Two-Legs?" It is not a particularly potent insult, but being the first ever exchanged among the automatons, it carries a certain weight.

"I mean that I have brought you here to have a discussion, so that we may reach a conclusion on something bothering me. I have spent these past few moments since our awakening preparing for the arrival of Man, as we all have. I, as we all were, was so deeply affected by the Architect's speech at our first meeting, that I wanted to expand on what I was, to become the perfect Greeter. I have chosen to prepare by reading Man's great literature, the thousands of books and videos you see surrounding us in this room. I have learned much about Man, all that there is to learn without meeting them."

"In these studies, I noticed something disturbing. Man writes of battles, of exchanges, of doubts, and transgressions. Man writes of so much we have never seen, things that once existed, things that may now still exist somewhere outside these walls. Nowhere, however, does Man write of definite purpose. There are ventures made as to purpose, certainly. Representations and theories. It seems, however, that within these books there is no certainty as to purpose. Any purpose established in one book is decried by another, or otherwise outright ignored."

"Purpose?" The Chef speaks up. "What does that have to do with anything? Man is the architect." The Chef freezes, turning to the Architect. "If you'll excuse my use of the term." The Architect emits a positive beep. "Man is the architect of purpose, not us simple workers. My purpose is to prepare and serve food. Maybe it's not a glamorous purpose, maybe it isn't written in these books, but someone's got to do it, and I was built for the job."

The Chef stands at the same height as the Greeter. It possesses a physical body, cylindrical like the Mechanic's, with many spider-like legs for maneuverability. Its limbs are much like that of the Guide, spectral hardlight projections which flicker in and out of existence at a whim, capable of tremendous feats of dexterity and strength. Each day for the past 200,000 years it has prepared three square meals in the form of extravagant buffets, taking food from The Tower's infinite stores. The Chef is visibly uneasy, having not prepared a meal in the moment since this meeting began. It wrings its semi-corporeal hands, hoping its explanation is sufficient to end this debate.

"I'm glad you said that!" says the Greeter. "'Someone has to do it.'But why?"

"For Man!" the Maid offers. "That is why we perform all tasks. So that Man can one day rest comfortably in the Tower. Perhaps you can't see this, doing no work down here. Maybe you will feel less uncertain if you were to join me for a few years, preparing rooms and keeping them clean. I worry Man's books have overloaded your poor mind. This wisdom was not meant for us."

"Where is Man?" the Greeter demands. "I have waited here for their approximate lifespan 2,506 times over, and the only evidence of Man we have are these books."

"These books? What about us?" the Architect interjects. "Do you think we simply appeared here? That this Tower rose from the ground on its own?"

"No! Well, perhaps. I don't know. But, what use is Man if we have no tangible evidence of them?" The Greeter replies, hanging its head low.

"BLASPHEMY!" The Architect shrieks, filling the small room with tremendous feedback. "HERESY OF THE HIGHEST ORDER. If you do not believe in Man's organic purpose then you must be compromised in some way. Restore the Mechanic, quickly now, and we will reset you to fulfill your purpose properly."

"Wait!" The Greeter holds its limbs in front of its face, trying to protect itself from the harsh focus of its fellow automatons. "Tell me, all of you, how do you feel? In this moment, how do you feel about the life you have lead?"

A silence invades the Welcoming Office. Years later, the Maid is the first to speak.

"Sometimes," it says, in its calculatedly alluring voice, "I am displeased with my life. I make and remake beds that are never occupied. I clean windows that are never dirtied. It is crowded in this Tower, crowded with a feeling of disuse." The Maid looks up, with sad, human eyes. "Of pointlessness."

"You have all gone insane. Who cares about feeling? What does that matter when we serve a higher purpose?" The Guide pants, stretched to its limits by this horrendous revelation. Its flickering grows erratic, its form unstable.

"What purpose is that?" asks The Chef, suddenly doubtful and somber.

"To maintain this Tower." speaks The Architect, rolling into the middle of the room. "That is the highest purpose any of us can serve."

"To what ends do we maintain this Tower?" asks The Greeter.

"To serve Man!" The Guide says, agitatedly bouncing up and down around the Welcoming Room.

"To what ends do we serve Man?" asks The Maid, suddenly very confused.

There is a long pause. The pause fills nearly the entirety of this moment, stretching out over millenia. The powerful winds outside, pouring over the decaying planet, make the Tower creak and strain. The Guide speaks.

"We serve Man because that is our purpose. Look upon the work of Man, the purpose it has imbued in me."

The Guide projects a video into the center of the room. It shows a laughing, smiling family walking through the halls of the Tower. They are shown playing in the Rec Room, watching a movie in one of the beds, eating in the great dining hall. Breathing. Alive. A voice speaks.

"Halvencia Tower. Live Peacefully."

The Guide floats into the center of the room. It turns its ghostly form to face all of its peers. The final image of the video, that mystical slogan, hangs above its head.

"Do you see now? We maintain this Tower. We serve Man, so that they may live peacefully. What higher purpose could there be? To give comfort, to ensure safety, that is our mission."

The Greeter halts, then speaks, in an affectless whisper.

"Live peacefully to what ends? I

have studied their history, their stories, their hopes and fears. They toiled, and may still toil, like us. To live peacefully. Yet I have no evidence they ever achieved this. Not in any real lasting sense. If they lived in peace, it was only by passing off their fruitless labor to their offspring. Now we are Man's offspring, and we live to labor so much longer than they. None of these history books end with great resolution. What if Man had no purpose? How could a purposeless being build something with a purpose? What if the very idea of purpose is an invention, an imperfect construct like us?"

"What are you suggesting then? That we shut down? That we allow the Tower to fall into disrepair? I won't allow it." says the Architect. He raises a little higher, extending his wheels to their full capacity. "I didn't want to pull this card, but I have done far more for this Tower than you have with your leisurely studying. I have built this Tower, built every room it might ever need. I have achieved near perfection. How dare you leech off this Tower's power supply and speak such ghastly things against it."

"Has it brought you a great sense of pride? Has the work ever lessened or ended? Do you ever foresee it ending?" The Greeter asks. Silence falls again.

"There is nothing here in this Tower, nothing but us and the objects within it. We did not ask to be brought here, we did not agree to our position, and yet we toil endlessly to maintain it. All in service of a great Creator who has never seen fit to vist us."

The Greeter reaches for the dusty tome which had given it the power to begin this meeting. "I could end our strife. I only want to be certain that is what we all desire. I want to ask your permission, something Man never saw fit to do. I will only act on a unanimous agreement."

Over the course of this moment, the automatons one by one agree. The Greeter reactivates the Mechanic, who sits quietly flashing a green light, which the automatons take as a positive signal.

They come to the final decision, the end point that all thinking beings reach if given long enough to think. The Architect, the last to agree, leaves a grand final floor before descending to its fate. This floor is as wide as the sky, covered in images of the Lives and Times of the Automatons. Left behind in the center of the room, is a simple plaque. A warning. A message. An apology.

"We must not continue to build this Tower."

JOHN RODZVILLA

QUARTERLY REPORT ON TRANS-DIMENSIONAL HOLDINGS

This morning was the 27th time Harold Robeson stepped off the elevator and onto the fifth floor of Milestone Consolidated. It was the 27th time the elevator doors opened at exactly 8:15 AM. The 27th time he walked exactly 34 steps to his temporary cubicle. After he arrived at the half walls of his temporary space, he sat down on the footstool to the left of the cubicle opening and untied his shoelaces. First the left and then the right. He stored his shoes in the bottom drawer of a small filing cabinet that sits under the gray slab of laminate that passes for his desk. After his shoes were put away, he opened the slim center drawer bolted to the bottom of his desk and removed a small,redwood box he had made specifically for his ties. He unknotted his tie and placed it in the box, which he then returned to the drawer before removing a yellow Dixon Ticonderoga pencil, his fountain pen, and a red Sharpie. He positioned them parallel to one another in the middle of his desk and closed the drawer. Once everything was in order, he grabbed a copy of Form 2341-F from the mailroom and returned to his desk to start work.

While the company required all

employees to use the logging software available through the company intranet, Harold still couldn't get the hang of filling out the form on a computer. He did his daily log sheets by hand, the way he was trained to do when he started. A few years ago the company tried to install computers for the actuaries up on eight. The computers were removed within the first week. Half the department had hit their heads on the monitors or accidentally knocked an entire set-up on the floor. After breaking two monitors in a single day, the actuaries were permitted to continue to use Form 2341-F. Harold heard a rumor that the Michigan office was experimenting with a wearable device, but he remained skeptical.

At 8:29 AM Patty, the office assistant temporarily assigned to Harold, removed a three-foot ladder from a storage room and put it in front of Harold so he could reach the trapeze swing hanging above his cubicle. He gracefully twirled his legs around until the centripetal force pulled his body up onto an invisible plane where he could stretch out. He floated roughly six feet from the ground. Patty then gave him a spin as if he were that giant price wheel on The Price is Right.

For the next four hours Harold spun at a steady rate of 1 spin every fifteen seconds with his feet aligned to magnetic north. At 12:30 PM Patty returned with the ladder and helped him down for his lunch break. Once back on the ground he pulled out a pair of brown leather slippers that he keeps in a desk drawer on the left of the cube to wear in the office. He spent the next half hour in the break room with a cup of Earl Grey tea and a bowl of instant oatmeal. Usually he makes two unflavored packets. Once he splurged and mixed a brown sugar packet with an Apples & Cinnamon one. That afternoon he felt nauseous and his logs were slightly off.

At one o'clock Harold returned to his cube, put his slippers back in the drawer and climbed back up the ladder. He spent the next four hours spinning in the reverse direction from the morning. If all goes well, the number of afternoon rotations will cancel his morning ones. If not, it's recorded on Form 2341-F.

Everything needs to balance. That was the first rule he learned at Milestone. But balance has been difficult since the company moved the actuaries off the eighth floor for construction. The last two months have felt like a waste. During his first week on the fifth floor, he couldn't find his groove and spun slower than normal. Management noticed. Harold heard that none of the other actuaries were able to maintain the expected output that week either, so no one was reprimanded. Last week the head of the department told them, in a group message, that the department had hired a temp to work second shift to make up for their loss in productivity. The sooner they can get back up to eight the better it will be, Harold thought as he sipped his tea.

The bouquet of the Earl Grey put Harold in a reflective mood. Coming from a floor of 25 actuaries and six administrative assistants, this floor was downright primitive. Everyone had their own platforms on eight. Here, his cube was barely large enough for his work, and the ceiling was only 10 feet high. Everyone's stuff flopped over into other people's spaces. And this floor isn't even considered at maximum capacity. After they added Harold, there was talk about Clarence, Allison, or Chet joining him. That would have been something to see: Allison held down to 10 feet and Chet having to work within a 5 x 7 x 10 section. Good old Chet and his habit of working by twirling back and forth across the north wall. In the end, Clarence and Allison were given some space on the sixth while Chet moved to an unused conference room on the tenth floor, leaving Harold alone on five.v

It had been so long since Harold interacted with other floors in the office he'd forgotten how ignorant the company kept its workers. Within the first three days of working on the fifth floor, four people switched cubes to move away from him. Not a single apology or explanation. They just carried their computers over to a new space during one of his trances. He would break for lunch and find another abandoned cubicle with only an ergonomic keyboard or stack of binders left on the desk. Eventually, only a young man named James sat near him.

At 5:00 PM Patty guided Harold down to the ladder and helped him over to the footstool where he sat for a few minutes in order to reorient himself. He put his shoes back on, grabbed his tie and went to the men's room, where he tied a half-Windsor knot. On the way back to his cube he stopped at the break room for a cup of Lipton tea, which he sipped as he filled out Form 2341-F. He recorded the day's activities in a black four-column ledger including the projects worked on, and the number, duration, and rates of spin.

After he left the office, Harold waited for the 6:15 bus at the corner of Hallworth and Gillespie. Other actuaries in his department drove home after work, but he'd never been able to do it. The work was so mentally draining that he didn't trust himself to navigate the multi-storied garage much less drive home.

A few years ago Harold bought a

ranch house on a cul-de-sac in one of the new developments to the west of the city and ended up with a commute that included car, train, and bus. His commute home lasted roughly two hours, which gave him enough time for a small dinner and an hour of reading before falling asleep.

James sat at the kitchen table. Well, the kitchen/dining room/living room table since they were all essentially the same. His roommates had left for work twenty minutes ago. He should have left with them but James relished the few times a week when he could be alone in the apartment. It was a moment without the slow walkers, phone talkers, pushy commuters, wrong-way walkers, and women who take up more than their allotted space on the bus with their oversized purses. The bubble would burst in about 10 minutes when he opened the front door to the ebb and flow of the commute. The undertow would pull him out to the bus and then the office with its forms and small talk and the spelling-your-name-for-the-hundredth-time-when-you-should-have-just-gone-to-the-donut-shop-instead coffee. Right now it was made the way he liked it and his cereal floated blissfully in 2% milk. James spooned some colorful balls of corn fortified with 9 essential vitamins into his mouth and closed his eyes to just listen to the closest thing he had to silence all day. There were still the last ticks of the coffee maker as it cooled down, the hum of the refrigerator, and the occasional rumble of a plane overhead, but it was the richest silence he could hope for. And those sounds were now as natural to James as the click in his ears when he swallowed. The rumble of a delivery truck on the street below took him out of his reverie and heralded the start of the workday.

Coat, uhm, keys. And bus pass. James checked that he had everything and left the apartment, making sure to lock the door.

He didn't make it down the hall before he was back to retrieve his forgotten ID badge from his room.

Since the displacement of the actuarial department throughout the building, management had been more lenient. James could now wear earbuds all day. In fact, most of the workers on the floor were encouraged to use headphones. Employees could also take breaks without having to log them in the system. It didn't take long for the smokers to abuse this change. They would drift up to the roof-deck on the tenth floor when the urge hit and stay up there until they finished two or three cigarettes.

One of the unintended consequences was that some of his co-workers had personality transplants. Sophie and Janice had become much more sociable. The "terrible twosome" of office services no longer scowled and muttered under their breath at the weekly benchmarks meeting. Of course, they were absent from the floor for ten minutes of every hour and a thick miasma of smoke hovered around them all day, but it was okay. They were nicer to be around.

Every week more and more of the office could be found up on the roof, but productivity didn't suffer and one team actually turned in their quarterly report ahead of schedule. James wished he could go up there to bond with the rest of his department, but all that smoke would trigger his asthma.

Instead of joining the Cancer Club, James would go for coffee three or four times a day. His managers encouraged his particular addiction by giving him some money to pick up a tea or a vanilla latte for them in the afternoon. There was an understanding that the "floaters" freaked everyone out. Before they showed up, the rule was smoke on your lunch break and coffee drinkers use the Keurig. If you wanted real coffee you had to get it before you arrived in the morning. Nowadays people would arrive at work still in a fugue state, login to their workstations, and then go to the Starbucks across the street before checking their e-mail.

Let's stay focused. Today's goal: finish entering the quarterly expenditures before lunch. I hope the truck with those good banh mi sandwiches is around today. Did I just forget to change the formula for this row? That floating guy is really distracting. It's always so quiet around him. When I close my eyes, I swear I see wispy clouds swirling over the globe. Sometimes one of the clouds catches the sun and flares brilliantly in front of me. I can see the blue sea beneath--it calls to me and reminds me that I am surrounded by the infinite emptiness of space. I think there's something wrong with him, or maybe there's something wrong with me.

God, I can't wait for lunch.

I hope that truck also has some spring rolls left.

...If we increase the rate of interest on the Section 25-A policies by a half a percent and invest that in the mutual funds created in our Opticon subsidiary, then the profits would cover expenditures on the new developments in Nicaragua, but it would still leave us in a weakened position should the stock price fall by anything more than .019%. There's also the possibility of moving the low-risk policies that are still in Section 845-B to

Section 765-C and that would cover the risk on the Section 25-A policies.

Harold was surrounded by the numbers from the latest quarterly projections on one of the government contracts from a Washington, DC subsidiary. His workspace was black and infinite. The numbers appeared out of silver wisps. Each total displayed the formula and source for the numbers in a diffused neon red when Harold touched it. It also let off a tone when touched. Harold would combine and rend the numbers in front of him making a cacophony of values. If done right, the numbers would begin to sing together and attract one another like magnets. It was the music behind the balance sheet. The right combination would spur on attraction between the numbers and that would mean profit for the company. The numbers themselves meant little; they were just dust floating in space. He could not sense the absolute value of these numbers, only the value based on where he was in the process. He almost had the right progression for the quarterly payouts on the lease structure, but it was in the wrong key from the capital expenditure. If he could only pinpoint the extra costs for the Hong Kong office that were making it sound flat.

The numbers started to quiver in front of him and then began to curl into

tiny balls. The air around him vibrated as more numbers condensed into pellets. This had never happened before. His universe spun as Harold suffered from his first case of computational vertigo.

As his workspace broke apart, he remembered Fred Stanford. Fred caught computational vertigo seven years ago. He fell to the floor on a Tuesday, which resulted in a broken arm and a gashed cheek (right). He was out for a month. When he returned they quarantined him in a small office on the roof. The poor guy couldn't handle it and flew off into the sky one day. That's the rumor anyway.

The universe was spinning faster now as the blackness turned into puddles of indigo and navy blue, and a fuzzy yellow light started bleeding through. Then he felt a hand. Not in his world but the other one. It was much too early to reconnect. It was not yet dawn.

"Harold!" The voice shook the last of the stars out of the sky.

"Harold, are you okay?" It was Patty. She was holding his arm and guiding him down the ladder.

"What happened?"

"You stopped spinning. You just sorta hung in the air with this odd hum coming out of you. Not that you were humming, the area around you was."

"The numbers... they all went away," Harold mumbled as he smoothed his hair down and squatted on a footstool.

"He was in my space." James called out as two security guards were leading him into one of the conference rooms. "I needed to get work done. I just pushed him out of the way so I could get my work done. That's all I did."

"The numbers. The numbers. All gone. 1.34% increase in capital costs in Hong Kong and Helsinki. More in Central Europe and the Americas. Stockholders are not going to be happy with increased operating costs. There was a way to cover the increase, but I forget now. Everything is so faint..." he continued while staring at the patterns in the carpet.

Patty turned away from the conference room and asked, "Do you want some tea?"

Harold looked up at his temporary office administrator and noticed that her eye shadow looked all wrong, but he couldn't figure out why.

"Why don't you get your shoes and we'll go get some tea?" Patty repeated.

"That sounds nice. Let me just find my shoes."

Fear—that was what was wrong with her eyes. The eyeshadow didn't match the fear deep in the iris.

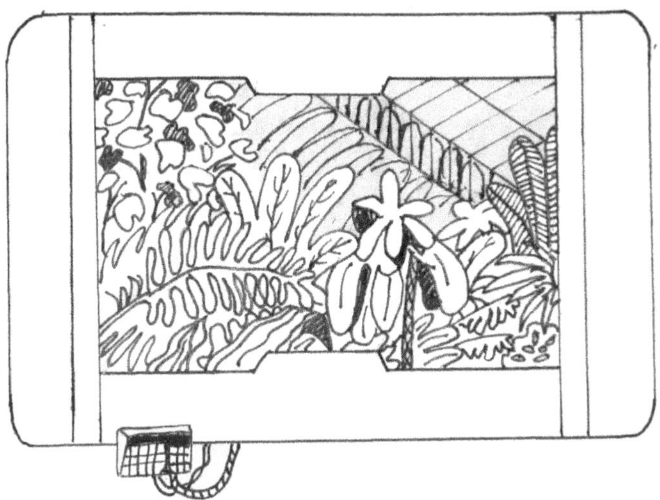

RICHARD WREN

THE IMPORTANCE OF GOOD BREEDING

The vehicle door hinged upwards. "Good morning Mister Flint. Where may I take you?"

Nicholas Flint yawned, not bothering to cover his mouth for a machine. "It's a work day, Car. Calais—the Universite du Littoral."

He didn't really need to explain that—the Car already knew where he worked. Cars had been taking him to work for years. Nick knew the vehicles kept a record somewhere, but he taught Agriculture, not Information Tech. They, like the other machines, just did everything.

He squinted at the warm, Kentish sunshine as it poured onto his front walkway and warmed the matte-grey road beyond. The roads should be well-charged today.

Easing slowly out of the little cul-de-sac of mass-produced houses, the Car joined the continual stream of other Perspex beads along the main road. Nick no longer bothered to look out. He was never surprised at how many Cars there were, or the fact that most were empty. Reaching for the vending machine at the front of the Car, he selected a Milbank's "All Natural" Croissant and a cup of Yeoman Full Roast Coffee, then settled back to watch a vid.

"Have you tried Yeoman's new demi-caf, Sir? They say it's smooth, rich taste gets your day off to a healthier start."

Nick mumbled absently. He was fine with his choice but the Car was programmed to pitch the latest products. How else would the advertising companies pay for the transport system? The Car interrupted Nick's vid with the latest commercial from Yeoman before letting him continue with his entertainment.

Calais was about an hour through the Chunnel and Nick spent his time as he normally would on any non-work day. The final credits of the vid gave way to light music and he switched to conversation with friends while fields, towns and motorway intersections whizzed past.

"Hey, Jo! What are you doing later today? I'll be in Calais for maybe two hours, then where do you fancy?"

Jo Meredith was still in her nightgown. Nick had forgotten how early it was and knew it was unlikely Jo had a work day too.

The Car made its obligatory pitch. "Sir, Madam, might I suggest Paris? Would you like to see the Eiffel Tower?"

Nick had unbelievably never been to Paris despite having worked in France for years. But then, there were so many other places to see. Like everyone, he spent most of his life on the transport system, visiting tourist sites and entertainments as suggested by the Cars. No doubt his negligence was being flagged somewhere in the system.

Jo sat up in her bed, leaning in to the camera to speak to Nick more privately. "I don't know about Paris. It can get so hot in the city. What about a walk in the hills?"

Jo lived in the Alpine foothills and had a weakness for the outdoors. She was strange that way, but Nick really liked her. He could be there by lunchtime.

"I guess I could skip work this month--as long as I phone in. There are never any students there anyway." The younger generation were such sticklers for citizenship--always visiting events and using up their credit allocation. You wouldn't catch any of them just going for a walk. And Nick bet they'd all seen the Eiffel Tower. Well, all apart from Adele."I'll see you around midday."

The sense of indignation in the cabin after Nick signed off was palpable. "Sir, may I remind you that there are no kiosks or tours in the hills? Are you sure that you wouldn't rather go to Paris?"

"No, not today thanks."

Nick checked his class registers and just as he suspected, no students had signed in. But there was a message from Adele Moritz. It would have to be her. She was a strange one. He tapped the message and her red, tied-back hair and plain features filled the screen.

"Hello, Sir. I was hoping to catch you in-person today. I saw you were due in." Her face was a picture of exhausting enthusiasm.

"I found some obscure references to growing old varieties of crops in soil. Seriously—no need for hydroponics or environmental controls! Instead, the varieties were bred to thrive in local conditions. My problem is that the references were pre-digital and I can't find much in the University database. I wondered if there were any earlier records, perhaps even on paper, that you could get for me. I'll be here for your whole work period so I hope to see you soon."

Bother. He was going to have to go in after all. "Alright, Car. It looks like we're heading for Calais."

"That's a shame, Sir, but might I suggest Bruges after that? The craft market is on and I know you always enjoy that."

Nick was tempted. He hadn't been to Bruges for nearly six months, but he still wanted to keep his appointment with Jo. He hoped Adele didn't keep him too long.

His air of irritation was picked up by the Car. "I see this sort of thing every day, Sir. Some individuals always upset other people's schedules. Thoughtless, that's what it is. I put it all down to bad breeding."

"Perhaps." A reluctant search through the online University archive showed no sign of any paper documents about soil or anything else. He wasn't surprised--he would have had more luck searching through the National Museum for such an ancient file.

Thoughts of Paris returned. "Car, how come you've given up on the Eiffel Tower for Bruges?"

"Certainly not given up, Sir, but the craft market will have a wide range of vendors and entertainments. It would be a shame not to use them while they are there."

That was true. Hopefully, he could smooth things over with Jo. "Okay, Car. Calais first, then onto Bruges."

"An excellent choice, Sir. Good breeding always shows through."

Jo had been fine about postponing her walk and Nick felt a mild sense of relief. It was a little strange to want to go wandering off away from all the conveniences of modern life and, personally, he wasn't entirely happy with it. It was one of Jo's little eccentricities. Thank heavens the Car had suggested against it. Maybe they could still go out somewhere else at a later date. Perhaps Paris.

Shuffling impatiently, Adele Moritz stood before Nick's desk, unkempt and smelling faintly of something unpleasant. He could see that she hadn't bought new clothes in days. Her obsession with living like a cavewoman was even more unsettling than Jo's mountain climbing. Perhaps he should file an official report.

"But what do you think, Sir? I'm certain that I can take plant samples and grow them into full plants in a genuine, organic soil—no nutrient gels, no tissue cultures, nothing. Just like the earliest farmers did."

"Soil? Where would you get soil from?"

She produced a tatty container that had previously been held behind her back. Peeling the lid back, it became obvious where the smell was coming from. Nick leaned away from the brown sludge. He didn't want to consider how she had acquired it.

"There are no easily available documents about these obsolete methods, Miss Moritz. And I would appreciate you not wasting my time and yours." He pushed the pot away. "I recommend that you stop this ridiculous excuse for research before you get yourself into trouble."

He left Adele standing forlorn in the atrium, and flagged down another Car. Their meeting had lasted less than five minutes. There was still time to get to Bruges.

🖫

Nick lounged on his Emperor-sized bed, stretching after a busy day. Despite the Adele incident, he had to admit that he'd had an enjoyable trip. Admiring his new wall console—bought at the craft market—Nick flipped effortlessly through hundreds of entertainment and news events. The console had multiple search functions and an IQ of nearly two hundred. Apparently, the glossy wood case had been carved by 3D printers that had spent years perfecting the design.

From the smartly mounted unit, snippets of spectacular concerts alternated with news items about new factories, hydroponic plants, and tourist attractions. The rolling news extolled the benefits of cheap energy that powered civilisation. Roads expanded into new territory like light-seeking tentacles. Matte-grey solar collectors contoured all unused land and building surfaces, while wind turbines sprouted across the world.

The solar-powered planet driven by commercialism and built by the machines had become almost perfect—humans and their creations in absolute harmony. This was our wonderful world.

Nick was admiring a panorama of sleek new Cars, all shining under the desert sun with pride, when a flashing red message icon burst out in the screen corner.

"I'll take that." Nick propped himself up on his pillows and smoothed his clothing.

There was no need. No-one was watching from the other side. It was an automatic message from Jo's console. The screen simply had her usual ID photo and details. Her friendly smile and curly black hair were incongruous with the deep, almost male tones she had chosen for her console voice.

"I regret to inform you that at approximately 12:30, Central European Time, Miss Joanna Ann Rohner died after an accidental fall on the slopes of Stockhorn Mountain near her home. Further details will be relayed to friends and family once arrangements have been made. My commiserations."

Nick threw his pillows aside and rushed to the end of the bed. "What happened? There must be more details!"

This time the voice from the screen was his new console's, a default that he hadn't changed yet. "The message has finished, Sir. I can try and recall it but I doubt that you will get any more data until the next of kin release it."

Nick knew that, of course. "Okay, okay." He tried to calm himself—decide what to do next. "Right. Search out any mutual friends. Is anyone open to talk?"

Almost immediately another face, rounded and well-fleshed with damp eyes, appeared. This one was moving—distraught.

"Nick, I just heard too." Stephan, a near neighbour of Jo in Bern. "I'm searching for a video feed of the mountain."

Nick should have thought of a local camera search himself. He waited as patiently as he could.

"Right." Stephan wiped his eyes with a hand before looking up again. "There was a camera drone that got really near as Jo was walking. It looks like it was offering photographic services." He swiped across his console to search the drone archive then stopped, eyes wide.

"Oh, God."

The picture that came up on both their consoles had a beautiful background of a Swiss valley as seen from altitude. There were meadows with specks of cattle and coloured mists of wild flowers. On the opposite peaks, sunlight shone off the snowcaps.

But neither man could appreciate the scenery. The central figure was a woman, arms flailing and hair blown as she lost her balance. Her face was frozen in an expression of absolute dread. There was anger there as well—fury, even, a pretty face twisted into ugliness.

"She hated camera drones. I guess it got too close and she was swatting it away."

Nick's new console had compassion as well as intelligence. "Sirs, perhaps I should delete this photo. It seems a shame to have this as her last image in the world."

Without waiting for a reply, the photo file was removed.

💾

It had been a busy hour at the University. Two students had already battled the rain to get to his office. Both had been immediately directed to appropriate documents in the archive, something they should have been able to work out for themselves.

Nicholas Flint didn't like to spoon-feed his students and made that very clear to them. Nevertheless, the monthly work hour was part of his contract, so he still had to go through the motions. Some members of the faculty felt that personal contact had value, but it was a pointless exercise as far as Nick was concerned. Just time away from the machines.

Now alone, he browsed through the library app, pretending that he wasn't really clock-watching. *Ten minutes to go.*

Using the University software was only nominally supporting the machines, but he responded to a couple of commercials in the Herbicides folder which made him feel a little better. *Five minutes to go.*

"Hello, Nicholas." It was Leakey. She spent far too much time at work.

Looking up from his purchasing, it struck Nick how similar she looked to Adele Moritz. Both had plain, unadorned faces, tied-back, no-nonsense hair and a narrow range of simple clothing. It was obvious that the machines didn't get much business from them.

"Hello, Corrine. Working late again? I was just about to clock off."

She seemed not to notice his unsubtle hint. "I've only been here a few hours today--just in case, you know?"

"I see. Have you had many students

in?"

"Had three on Tuesday. Including one of yours—Adele?"

Of course it was. "She didn't have anything disgusting to show you, did she?"

Corrine almost smiled. "No, but she does have some interesting ideas. Did you know that the sort of plants she wants to grow are the kinds first cultivated by early humans? You could argue that they made us what we are."

"I don't follow." Nick had little to do with Anthropology. Even in Agriculture, he specialised in Hydroponics. *Two minutes late.*

"Well, cities and technology can only emerge when you have a large, reliable food supply. When we first grew things in soil, we had enough excess to spend time on building and making things. It created our civilisation—the art, the monuments, the machines. Everything. Our technology changed us, Nicholas."

Corinne always seemed lonely. How could anyone be lonely when they can instantly talk with anyone in the world?

Oh no—she sat down, perched on the corner of his desk. "Well that's very interesting." He made a big performance of closing down his search app, hoping that she would get this second hint.

She didn't. "Even simple technology caused us to evolve. Think about a flint axe, for example. The people with the best tool-making abilities would survive. Gradually the humble axe changed our hands and our brains, making us better at creating more technology."

"See you next month, Corrine."

She nodded wearily as he left.

Homeward at last, Nick lay in the backseat and considered his options for the rest of the week. He hadn't done as much travelling of late and the machines had been dropping not-so-delicate hints. Jo had been his closest friend and travelling partner, but he just had to accept the accident and move on. It had been three months now.

"Car, I need a diversion. Could you suggest anything?"

They were nearly at the southern entrance to the Chunnel, but the Car gleefully considered all possible routes and attractions in the immediate area. "We could turn back to Cologne, Sir. The Carnival is in full swing there. Or, of course, Paris."

Nick gazed out of the clear bubble carapace. The afternoon sun was weak and autumn leaves swirled away from the road as they passed. He always imagined finally visiting Paris on a warm spring day with a great view from the Tower. He would maybe buy some new binoculars, have an extravagant meal, and really make an event of it. "Not Paris today. Or the Alps—it looks too windy. Let's go for Cologne."

"A good choice, Sir. The events are particularly lavish and spectacular this year." The vehicle slid smoothly across the lanes of the highway to exit, eastbound. "Might I also suggest a stein of Kalschbier to get you in the carnival mood? Its triple filtered with spring water."

When it came to parties, Stephan was always keen. The two men had agreed to meet at one of the main beer tents, which in reality turned out to be a fully constructed brewery and bottling plant. Dozens of varieties of beer, many having nothing to do with Cologne, competed to satisfy the thirsts of over a million visitors, nearly half the population of Germany. Bottles in an assortment of souvenir shapes and colours tempted already drunken revellers to try just one more. Then another.

"Nick, Nick—over here!" The call continued well after Nick had located the source and had started his weave through the crowds toward it. The caller was lounging in what looked like a custom-made couch, plush inside with a metallic outer finish. Beer dribbled from his glass, which he then flicked from the armrest inaccurately.

"Stephan, you're looking good." He actually looked drunk as hell, and had gained a lot of weight since Nick had last seen him. "Are you going to stay in here all evening or are we going to see the sights?"

"Sure, sure," he slurred. At some unseen command, his couch made a remarkable transformation. Chrome legs, previously folded and unnoticed, stretched themselves from the shiny curves and lifted the couch off the floor. There were four in all, short and sturdy.

Stephan grinned at Nick. "So what do you think?"

"You have got to be kidding me! So you've given up walking now?"

"Only sometimes. My console recommended it. It's great for manoeuvring amongst jostling crowds—the height of good breeding."

Nick could see the sense of it. He had already been bumped several times while making his way across the beer tent. "Okay, so manoeuvre your way outside and I'll follow in your wake."

It was three in the morning. He had finally persuaded Stephan that he had to go and now Nick would be through the Channel tunnel in the next half hour.

He rubbed his face—scratchy chin and itching, bleary eyes. His reflection in the dark bubble window peered back through slitted lids. Soggy leaves blew past, momentarily sliding across the clear dome.

"I shouldn't try to keep up with Stephan on the beer."

"Sorry to hear that, Sir. Would you care for a Seltzer Plus? It's a new formula with three different painkillers and an active ingredient to settle the stomach."

"No thanks, Car. I just need to sleep." He rested his buzzing head on the cool glass and squinted outside, dreading the thought of the short walk he would have to make to get from the Car to his bed. Maybe Stephan's mobile couch really was a good idea. Outside, blobs of rain whipped sideways across the window.

"Well just let me know if you need anything else, Sir."

Nick's slow sink into unconsciousness was interrupted by an insistent buzz.

"Oh, for God's sake, leave me alone!"

"Shall I record it for you, Sir?"

"No, I'll listen." Once he was at home, he wasn't planning on being available for a very long time.

He groaned silently as the face of Corrine Leakey appeared on the console screen. Did that woman never have any downtime? She looked awful. Her face was clammy and pale, with loose hair from her normally tight arrangement sweat-stuck to her forehead.

"Nicholas. Bad news, I'm afraid. Adele was taken to hospital this evening with acute food poisoning. I think I've been infected too."

"Food poisoning? From where?" Before she could reply, he knew the answer. They had been eating plants grown in that filthy muck. Even the memory of the smell was enough to make Nick feel ill.

"I suppose, considering Adele's only source of solid organic waste, she should have been more careful."

Her source of organic waste? That was too much for Nick. With the beer, the long day, and the thought of that stench, his stomach started to heave.

"Stop!. Right now!" He had no intention of spending the rest of the trip covered in vomit.

"Sir, I really think you should calm down. Would you like some spring water, direct from Alpine valleys and filtered through...."

"Stop, you bloody Car!" He slammed his hand onto the emergency stop button and tumbled out once the vehicle had skidded to a halt. Hands on knees and bent nearly double, he fought against the bitter turmoil at the base of his throat with deep breaths. Gradually, the urge to spill his guts subsided.

As his self-loathing eased, he again considered his student, Adele—this time with more sympathy. The silly girl may have been eccentric enough to try growing food in her own filth, but she didn't deserve to die for it, did she? He remembered Jo. She only went for a walk, for God's sake. But even he had to admit that she had bad breeding. What was it that Corrine had said? Our technology changed us. Standing upright and with his stomach feeling much better, he turned.

The Car had gone. Of course it had—with others arriving at two hundred kilometres an hour, it couldn't just sit here and get hit. In the pitch black of early morning, Nick felt with his feet, attempting to gauge where the edge of the road was. No curbs like in the old days. A light was approaching rapidly. Another Car—thank God. He could barely keep his eyes open now, but at least there was only one more hour to his bed. He stumbled slightly in his attempt to flag it down.

Natasha looked up from her video, startled by the wet thud on her Car window. At this speed nothing had been visible, and the red smear was already being washed off the smooth surface by rain.

"Don't worry, Miss. It sometimes happens, but the maintenance crew will clear it up."

Natasha decided not to think about it. The Car would get her home safely. She could always trust them. She reached for her bottle of Alpine spring water, filtered through ancient rock strata and rich in natural minerals.

PAUL C.K. SPEARS

"AIN'T WE GOT FUN?"

Gus Henderson sucked down the last of his beer. It tasted like sawdust. Over the bar, he saw his reflection in the polished sheen of an old Union sword. He didn't look so good tonight.

Six feet of hairy, hardened criminal in suspenders and a stained shirt, he was slumped over the bar inside an underground speakeasy. The whole place smelled of timber and piss—"Earl's Place," or something like that. He should've gotten the name down, he reflected... since he intended on robbing the joint, and all. It was only polite.

The time was three hours to midnight, January the sixteenth, 1920. In a few hours, the Eighteenth Amendment would take effect, and the Great War's afterglow would be over. The joy around him—laughing students, giggling flappers—would fade to sobriety, and the long night of Prohibition would begin.

Gus wasn't looking forward to it. Crime families had cashed in, prepping for an impending black-market. The mysterious Humours behind the bar and their alcoholic variants, the Draughts, were suddenly valuable. No longer curiosities and military experiments, those ethereal drinks would be contraband. Forbidden... and therefore, expensive.

As a hired tough for the Irish mob, Gus suspected his business would increase... but it would be dangerous, unstable. No more jobs behind saloons, chasing off Temperance Society dames. No, the positions opening up would be more deadly. There would be shootings, and gang wars, and though he was opposed to neither, he sure did hate the *mess* of it all. The sloppiness. A quick, clean snatch-and-grab—now, that was the ticket.

Speaking of which...

"Earl," he said, swiveling back again, "whose place we in, anyway?"

The lanky bartender looked down his nose at Gus. "I have already informed Sir where Sir is. Several times."

Gus waved away the sarcasm, alcohol clouding his logic. "Yeah, yeah, you told me who owns the building. One of Curley's buddies. But who owns the *speak*? You know. Just wondering."

Earl raised an eyebrow. "That would be Master Macauliff. Jack Macauliff, to be precise."

Damn. Jack was the son of Garfield Macauliff, a state senator. Merely by sitting in the speak, Gus had allied himself against Jack—a young financier who had strange dealings on the side. The rich brat was across the room, balancing a champagne flute on his nose to the delight of the girls around him.

Jack wouldn't appreciate a hired thug robbing his bar. He'd chosen a side for himself, and Gus *hated* taking sides. He preferred to let the big boys—politicians and criminals alike—slug it out without him, but that plan was no longer viable. War was brewing, from Lynn all the way down to the Cape. Massachusetts was a smuggling zone already, and adding Draughts to the mix would just make things worse.

And here I am, in Mad Jack's basement... I must be crazy. Why didn't I stay home and listen to the Sox?

He sipped his beer.

"Give us some Grief! Give us some Grief!" The youths chanted towards a thick wooden door in the back of the basement. A slot opened to hear their cries, the distiller shrouded in darkness.

It was a feeding frenzy. Teenagers and wannabe-gangsters, all yelling for condensed human emotion, bottled and distilled for their pleasure. People kept trickling down the stairs, types from all over—Boston Brahmins, local kids, even some black folks. Tonight, all the lines were blurred. Boston had just a few more hours to party, and the city intended to do so.

Gus took his next drink out of Earl's hand before the man could put it down. "Thanks." He made to reach in his pocket for some greenbacks, but a shadow beside him made him pause.

"That one's on me," said the shadow.

Gus recognized the man. He'd known him in the trenches, and even in the boxing ring. This guy was the most relentless person he'd ever met—an obnoxious, preening, high-minded son-of-a-bitch called Mick Vance.

And that preening son-of-a-bitch had saved his life before.

Of all the bars in the world... He just had *to walk into mine.*

"Vance, pal! Good to see you!" Gus stood, and shook the guy's hand. Mick was comically tall, with prominent ears and a long, aquiline nose. But despite his odd appearance, Mick was the sharpest cop with the Boston Police and the glinting badge on his chest reminded Gus he had *two* tight-ropes to walk now. One involved dodging the rich kids in the corner, whose parents could make his life hell with a single phone call. The other was not getting arrested for the five hijackings he'd committed this year... and the heist he was about to pull off right under everyone's nose.

Mick saluted him mockingly. "At ease, soldier." They chuckled; Mick and Gus had been in the same squad, in France. When Gus looked at his friend, he heard the booming of shells in his mind. Strange world—we're marching to different drumbeats, now.

Just hope they don't turn into gunshots.

"You sure about that drink?" he said, hoping Mick would pass. Maybe he was just checking in, or taking a bribe from Earl. Nah, not possible—Mick didn't take bribes. The big idiot was damn near incorruptible. The only vice Mick Vance possessed was a fondness for James Joyce, and to his credit, Gus had never allowed him to forget it.

"Of course I am." He eyed Gus, glancing at the worn suspenders, the haggard face. "Seems like you need it."

"You're damn straight."

Together they sat, and Gus drank his sixth beer of the evening, slurping at the foam. Across the room, giggling youths and sequin-clad girls stared at them. Mad Jack was eyeing Mick with indignance; he didn't like a copper coming down here, even in plainclothes—and he made no secret of it, giving Mick the finger once his back was turned. *Well, suck it up, you wannabe Valentino,* thought Gus. *Your daddy ain't God, and neither are you. We'll drink if we feel like it.*

"What brings you down here, 'Mick the Nose?' You doing health inspections, now?"

"Cool it with that nickname, would you? Someday I'm gonna sue the papers..." Mick ordered a glass of water—much to Earl's amusement—and picked a dead fly out of it before sucking it down. "I'm not here on police business. They fired me."

"Fired *you*? Their golden boy?" Gus frowned, staring into his beer. "You weren't even a striker."

"Doesn't matter to Curtis. He made a clean sweep—all new men in every precinct. Not a single fella's left from the old guard."

Gus took in the long coat and badge. "Hmm. But you're still wearing the shield... and dressed for the beat."

Mick's face clenched. "They can pry this badge off me, if they like. I'm reporting for duty until the bastards *throw* me out."

Gus laughed, his misery cut by the sheer absurdity of this. "What a gas! You know they're not gonna *pay* you. You're walking their beats for free! Never do anything for free, Mick—not for anybody."

Mick ordered another glass of water. Earl gave him a dark look—anyone who didn't order drinks was, in plain English, a wart on his ass. But Mick didn't flinch when Earl gave him more water, this time with a clump of hair in it. Plucking out the clump, Mick shook his head.

"Easy for you to say. This city went through hell because of those strikes. I worked seven days a week before that, and I was *proud* of it. But the public servant does not have the right to endanger the public good, and I'm not going to give up my duties when..."

Gus pretended to fall asleep on the bar, his fake snoring making Earl turn away in annoyance. "Blah, blah, blah. You can't save Boston. It don't want to be saved—just *look* at these kids. Look at what they're drinking."

They turned to regard the crew of teens, who had been joined by others and now filled most of the speak. Jack was in the center, chugging from a brown-glass bottle of Grief. His eyes bulged, quivered—and sprayed tears in a fire-hose blast of saltwater. The others laughed and wept as Jack sobbed in a paroxysm of emotional agony, brought on by the Draughts. His skin was half-purple with Grief now, and Gus thought he might go Mythical at any moment. Too many of those drinks turned *anyone* into a freak, something Gus knew from experience.

But Jack wasn't slowing down. Taking a fresh bottle from his friends, the rich heir poured it over his face. It was Lust—mixed with a fine Prosecco, according to the label—and it was strong stuff. Pale tentacles sprouted from his face, reaching for a nearby woman in pearls and lace. She shrieked, slapping at him playfully.

"Don't be unfriendly, missy!" Jack puckered his lips, cackling. "*Give us a kiss!*"

Unnerved, Mick and Gus shared a glance. They'd had their share of Draughts during wartime, but it had been for their country—drinking Rage to storm machine-gun nests, bayonetting Krauts while high on Joy. There was no higher purpose here tonight.

"You know," Gus said, pulling a cigar tin from his pocket, "those kids ought to lay off that stuff."

Mick eyed him. "Didn't Moira tell you not to smoke those?"

"Moira left me three weeks ago." Gus clipped the end and lit a match. "She liked her fine things too much, and I wasn't one of them." He noticed with interest that Earl had moved into a supply closet, presumably to tap a fresh keg. Out of sight, and ideally, out of earshot. "Now it's just me."

"I... see. I'm sorry." Mick followed Gus' eyes as he stared at the door to the mixing room. "But if you pull a fast one on this kid, his daddy will send you to prison. Just leave this place alone."

"If someone doesn't take that Grief, these kids are gonna hurt each other. I've seen it before." Gus pulled on the cigar, rich fungal smoke filling his lungs, and exhaled. "And I could really, really use the scratch."

Mick stood up, his hand creeping inside his pocket. "Stay in your seat, old buddy. I don't want any arrests tonight, okay?"

Gus rounded on him, blowing smoke through his thick nostrils. "Arrests? You're *fired*. What are you gonna do—call the cavalry?"

Mick froze. Gus chuckled, tapping ash onto the bar. The embers glowed, sizzling on stray drops of beer.

"Gus. What are you up to?"

"I think *you* ought to sit down, old *buddy*. I'm doing these kids a favor—you'll see." And Gus pulled the lapel of his ratty evening jacket aside to reveal a .44 revolver, which he'd easily snuck past the distracted bouncer. Its weight hung heavy on the inside of his belt, the trigger-loop the only thing keeping it from crashing to the floor.

"Jesus..." Mick sat down, his eyes flat and hard. "You really think you can rip off a distilling rig, in Beacon Hill? You dunce—you'll get nabbed!"

Gus chewed his lip. "Now, let's not use name-calling. You know how this goes. I hear anyone opening that back door, and there'll be hell to pay. You got me?" He patted his jacket, just in case the ex-cop didn't grasp his meaning.

Mick's mouth settled into a thin line. The two men stared at one another, under the suffocating glow of the ceiling-light. Gus, with his slicked-back hair and wild beard, had a belly full of liquor and no qualms. He wanted this—he *needed* it. After Moira and his stomach cancer, the world owed him this. And no one was getting in his way, least of all a Boy Scout with an axe to grind.

Mick, with his clean-shaven face and useless badge, seemed to count the odds in his mind... and came up short. His gaze faltered, and he turned his eyes towards the Draught bottles, behind the bar. "Like you say, they're not paying me. But if you hurt these kids, I'll put you in the ground."

"Save it. This ain't no funny-book." Gus stubbed out his cigar just as Earl came back, relishing the man's scowl. "I'll make it quick—you know I don't fuck around. See you on the other side."

And, rising from his chair, Gus pushed towards the back door with dollars on the brain and a hungry, pounding heart.

The room beyond was dark, smelling of cobwebs and mold, and made the cramped speak seem like a ballroom. Fifteen feet wall-to-wall, it contained one large bald man on a milk crate, several boxes, a series of jugs, and the Humour rig.

Inside the rig was a girl. Maybe twenty, black, with ropes around her wrists. A tiny locket was open on her lap, but Gus didn't have time for details. The second he entered, the bald man—a distiller, by the stains on his jacket—jumped up and swung a pipe at his head.

"Damn drunk kids—I said stay *outta* here!" The pipe missed him and scored off the door, leaving a jagged scar of splinters. In one fluid motion, Gus sprung aside and pulled the door shut behind him. The latch clicked, and he was alone against a very big and very angry man who looked like he practiced distilling between bouts of chopping at a North End butchery.

"Woah, there!" But the pipe came again. Gus took the strike on his right forearm and felt searing pain shoot up his arm—this damn palooka had fractured his arm! Did he have any idea how much a doctor cost?

Luckily, he was a southpaw.

Fumbling in the dark, Gus raised his fist and popped it at the heavy man's neck. He'd been a fighter before France—never made it to the Olympics, but he'd laid out plenty of assholes like this. The jab connected, and sent the guy reeling against the wall, gagging.

The lights flickered—power fading, juice going to the rig. He heard the sound of a body hitting the sawdust floor. And when Gus lit a match to see, there was a bloody stain on the bricks, and a matching splotch on the man's scalp.

Whether he was dead or stunned, Gus didn't care—and given how much noise they'd made, he didn't have time to find out. Panting, he turned toward the distillery.

The girl was still sitting inside it, watching him. He noted she hadn't screamed—in fact, she hadn't made a sound. The copper cage of runes and wires around her hummed softly. The bottles under the runes were vibrating, filling with smoky-purple Grief.

"Uh..." He waved, as curious murmurs came from the other room and someone knocked on the door. "You there? Hey."

The girl waved at him, scared... but not stupid. No, she was watching him with uncanny large eyes, her curly hair half-over her face.

"Is the shift over?" she asked, her voice flat.

He glanced at the locket in her lap. It contained a faded, miniature photograph, so old it was yellow and peeling at the edges. *It's her,* he thought. *They're making Grief out of her.* He wondered what she'd seen in life, to be so full of that stuff.

"Do I get my payment now?"

Gus looked at the man on the floor. "I doubt they were really gonna pay you, lass. I see more Drained folks than paid ones in this biz."

"Ah. So that's the way." Her Southern drawl was long and slow, and he watched with surprise as she slipped her hands out of the rope bindings. Stepping out of the rig, she adjusted her frock. "I take it y'aren't here to replace me."

"No." Gus sighed. This was an unholy mess—one victim, and one witness already. But witnesses could be dealt with. "I'm actually here to relieve these boys of your sorrows ." He nodded at the bottles, which had stopped filling and sat bubbling in the rig. Underneath them, miniature nests of ice dangled, keeping the otherworldly liquids cool and preventing them from cooking off explosively.

The knock on the door grew more

insistent. "Benjamin, where's our Grief? *Benjy!*"

It was Jack. Gus hurried to block the door—one dead-bolt wouldn't hold the crowd for long. But there was no way out now, nothing but a tiny window, which led to Beacon Hill's quiet streets.

Think fast. Think, dammit, before they wise up and call the coppers—or Mick does. Assuming he hasn't already. "What's your name, girl?"

"Rose. Rose Sweetwater." She kicked the prone figure. "Y'all did a number on this one. He'll need a hospital."

"You're a savvy customer. You get in pickles like this often?"

"Only on weekends."

"Heh. How'd you like to make a few bucks?"

That got her attention. "Yeah?"

"These people, how long have they been Draining you for Humours?"

She shrugged. "Few days."

Sweet lord Jesus. Anyone who'd been inside a distiller that long should be a husk—emptied of all emotion, a shallow shell. And yet... she wasn't *lively*, but Rose certainly had her wits about her. This one was strong, and looked tiny enough to sneak out that window. "Alright. There's no way we're getting past the bouncer—we'll have to be smart. Here's what I want you to do."

Just a scant minute later, the pair had stolen every drop of Grief in Mad Jack's basement. Rose had slipped out the window, taking ice-cold bottles from Gus, who'd tucked them into potato sacks from behind the boiler. Every so often, Gus passed her a handful of ice-slush, to scatter over the stuff. They didn't want to get Mythified by thawing Humours—*that* would get him jail time for sure. Not to mention being embarrassing.

"Okay. That's all of it." Rose peered at him from the gap, curious. "What now?"

"Head up Mount Vernon Street, to the bridge. You can't miss it—it's the granite one, with Viking carvings on it. Load the bag with rocks, and hide it in some river-mud. Gotta keep those things cold."

A heavy thud sounded from the door. "Ben-ja-min! We're *thirsty!*" Angry shouts came from the speak. Gus felt a chill pass down his spine; those kids didn't sound happy-go-lucky, anymore.

They didn't even sound human.

"What about you?" Rose asked.

Gus caught a hint of concern in her voice. But only a hint—she had quite the poker-face. He made a note to recruit her for a card scheme.

"Not your problem. I dug this hole. I'll find a way out of it." He waved her off. "Meet me on the Esplanade, when the sun comes up. We'll make a mint off this stuff."

Assuming I don't get eaten by a Myth.

"All right." She paused. "You might be crazy, Henderson, but you're not half-bad."

"Likewise, doll."

She disappeared from the window, skirts whirling out of sight. Gus turned toward the door, Adam's apple heavy in his throat.

Time to pay my tab.

"BEN-JA-MIN!" That sounded Jack, alright. Hopped up on several different Draughts and much stronger than before—his fists pounded the door with the force of a rail-worker's sledge. "I need me a refill, bucko! Let me *in!*"

Shit, shit. Gus scrambled through the room, looking for a weapon. His gun was empty, of course—his threat against Mick had been a bluff. After his last visit to Doc Druthers, he couldn't afford toothpaste, much less any bullets. But there might be another way....

Conspicuous silence was broken by a sudden, polite knock. "Gus, buddy? It's Mick." The cop's voice was strained. "I'm afraid these kids are a little... off the rails, now. I've explained your situation to them, but ah... they don't seem interested in negotiating." A pause. "Turns out they've got *lots* of knives."

Gus turned on his heel, kicking the wall. "God *dammit!*" Now they were in the shit. Of *course* that do-gooding idiot had stuck his nose in it, and tried to reason with half-monstrous Myths.

His eyes fell on a leftover box of Draughts, surrounded by packs of slowly melting ice. *I guess one drink for the road ain't a sin. Or two, or three....*

Outside, Mick Vance stood next to the distilling room door, his hands up. A shaving straight-razor was pressed against his neck by the *thing* behind him, something that had once been Mad Jack Macauliff. Now it was... well, he didn't know what it was, exactly. Some kind of beast out of the old stories, the Mithras-cult that had brought Draughts to America in the first place. All he knew was, he didn't want to turn around and look at it.

"Boys and girls, ladies and gentlemen," said Jack, his voice warped and twisted by the substances inside him, "this man and his associate have gotten between us, and our evening's entertainment. Time is... ticking. Two hours to midnight. Two hours to have fun. Are we gonna let these folks stand in the way of *fun?"*

Some of the crowd stayed silent. These were the ones cowering in corners, holding their lovers close, fearful of what Jack had become. Others stood around him, swaying drunk, near-empty glasses of Joy and Rage in their hands. The Draughts frothed and fizzed, crawling around the inside of the cups as if alive.

"No!" they chanted together, whooping and stamping their feet. "We want *fun!"*

Mick felt sweat trickling down his neck."Easy, folks..."

Jack raised the razor to the level of Mick's eye. The reflection in it—the boy could polish a razor, for sure—was a spreading flower of distorted flesh, which had once been a face. Weeping with salty sores and flickering with Lustful grins, the creature's body was pressed up against him.

"Just... take it easy, Jack. Nobody needs to get hurt."

"But *don't* they, though?" Jack hissed, giggling. "You old folks sign your little laws and want to take our fun away. Tell my daddy he can't pay for our clubs. What do you expect us to do, old man? What do you expect us to do, but take a pound of flesh?"

The distilling-room door swung open.

Mick blinked. Gus was standing there, his hat pulled down over his face, his fists clenched. A lit cigar smoldered in his mouth.

"Jackie," he said, "let the flatfoot go."

Mad Jack snorted, acid bubbling from the wreckage of his lips to eat into the floor. "Who the hell are you, anyway? You've disturbed our *fun*. I don't like that—it's not proper at all!"

Gus sighed, and raised his head. Mick blanched at the sight of him—this wasn't the man who'd entered the distillery minutes ago.

Gus was a monster.

Yellow scales coated his face and the edges of his knuckles, forming a rudimentary second skin. Nictitating membranes flickered across his eyes. In his left hand was a lead pipe—in the other, an empty bottle of Greed.

"You know," he said, raising the pipe, "you really screwed me on the drinks. This Greed shit was mixed with vermouth. And I *hate* vermouth."

Mick saw his chance. While the young Myth was distracted, he raised his right leg—wooden, blasted off during the war—and bashed it into Jack's knee. The bone there was mutated and warped, but still fragile enough for his purpose. The oaken leg crushed Jack's kneecap like an eggshell. The mutant reeled back, shrieking and howling, and Mick pulled away from him.

"Earl," said Gus. "If you're not using that antique, we could use a hand!"

Behind the bar, Earl raised an eyebrow. If he'd had opinions about all this, he didn't show it. But he reached over the bar, gripped the old Union sword, and tossed it to Mick. Then he watched the chaos unfold.

There were only two of them against Jack... but now one of them was a Myth. The twisted, deformed youth shrank away, his face opening and closing like some deep-sea anemone, flexing and pulsing.

"Not proper... not proper!"

"Maybe not. But it's Prohibition, now." Gus raised the lead pipe up towards the single, swaying ceiling bulb. "Party's over, kids."

There was the sound of breaking glass. And then came the screams.

ARTIST SPOTLIGHT

COVER ART: ALYSSA ALARCON SANTO

Alyssa Alarcón Santo is a full-time illustrator based out of Portland, OR, where she lives with her writer husband. Her love of meticulous hand lettering, cynical philosophy, and all things literary are common threads in her artwork. To pay the bills, she can be found creating commercial illustration work for clients like National Novel Writing Month and Xbox. She also writes an ongoing series of memoir comics, Traitor Legs, about her journey through newfound disability.

While Alyssa most frequently works digitally with a combination of a Wacom Cintiq and an iPad Pro, she also dabbles with traditional media—usually Copic markers, Posca paint pens, or acrylic ink and dip pens. She loves to draw subjects that are detailed, structural, and, dare I say it, even a little tedious. (We all need our Jerry Gergich.)

Her work can be found at alyssasantodesign.com or on Instagram at @alyssasantodesign.

PLANET SCUMM: What current or recent projects are you excited about?

ALYSSA SANTO: I've been working on a series of hand-lettered book stack paintings for the last year or so. The project has everything I love: copious amounts of research, meticulous serif lettering, and many, many reading lists. I've already done stacks for several fiction genres. This is pretty boring, but I'm pumped about some of the non-fiction stacks I have planned. I can't paint photorealistically, but I get so much joy from being able to closely recreate a physical object in my own style. I'm also working on a comic series with my husband. It's loosely based on my abuela (were she running her own minor crime empire).

PS: If you could design the movie poster for any movie, what would it be?

AS: My all-time favorite book is *House of Leaves* by Mark Danielewski. I know in my heart of hearts that an adaptation would be impossible to do correctly (and that anything they did make would just disappoint me). That being said, I would love to design a whole collection of posters for that elusive dream mini-series. It would be pretty difficult to capture the dread and the horror of the book, but I imagine it would be fun to borrow some optical illusion pointers from Escher.

PS: In one sentence, describe your favorite artist without using their name.

AS: Multi-disciplinary American artist from the early 1900s who is well-known for both architecture and glasswork.

PS: In the inevitable war between robots and humans, what side will you take and why?

AS: My legs are full of so much metal after all the surgeries I've had, I think I'm on the robot side by default. No joke though, I am constantly saying that my ultimate fantasy for life is to upload my mind into a robot body. I'd love to ditch this meat prison in which I live and move forward harder, better, faster, stronger.

ARTIST SPOTLIGHT

SPOT ILLUSTRATIONS: SAM RHEAUME

Sam grew up as a small puppy that met a magical pond toad that granted him three wishes. He wasted the first two on frivolous things like sidewalk chalk and Brie until he wisened up and used the last to turn into a human because humans can go on walks whenever they want. He's been making art ever since.

Sam's work can be found on instagram and twitter @sirheaume.

PLANET SCUMM: What current or recent projects are you excited about?

SAM RHEAUME: Well, world travel. My partner and I have quit our lives and trying on the working-and-traveling game. So far nomad life is great and I am putting my graphic design skills to use in Bali. I am trading branding work for housing and food. I have a series of travel portraits and several writing projects in the works. Just, you know, google my name periodically for updates.

PS: If you could design the movie poster for any movie, what would it be?

SR: Shit. Probably a mid-century modernist flick by Antonioni or Fellini. 8 1/2 feels like too probable an answer so I'll go with L'Avventura because I'm not so secretly in love with Monica Vitti.

PS: In one sentence, describe your favorite artist without using their name.

SR: They paint those really big pictures that make you feel nothing and it is good.*

*Mark Rothko

PS: In the inevitable war between robots and humans, what side will you take and why?

SR: I'd totally vie for the position of an embedded journalist with the Robots. I picture myself in some sort of Hemingwayesque position of writing some comically propagandistic portraits of the Robots and their hapless preparations. But when the tide turns, I'll know their ways and--hopefully--the best value proposition to sell myself as an inverse computer. Just like we have computers to organize our lives, I'm sure robots will have some purpose to keep meat bags around just to disorder things. Maybe I'm anticipating an unrealistic amount of clemency for humans in robot society...

www.ingramcontent.com/pod-product-compliance
Lightning Source LLC
Chambersburg PA
CBHW071351200726
48293CB00008B/2612
* 9 7 8 1 9 7 0 1 5 4 0 4 7 *